A Sleepytime Book ™

Too Many Animals Sleep In My Bed

By
Judith Clark
Illustrated by
Lisa Haughom

To Devin,
A Beautiful young lady
I hope to meet you one
day soon, I hope you like
this story. I did.
mom's friend,
Love Kathy

Dedicated to Animals Everywhere

kidsbooks ®
Incorporated

Text Copyright © 1993 by Kidsbooks, Inc. and Judith Clark
Illustrations Copyright © 1993 by Kidsbooks, Inc.and Lisa Haughom
3535 West Peterson Avenue
Chicago, IL 60659

I go up to my bedroom every night,
Fold down the covers, then turn out the light.

And always discover I can't rest my head,
'Cause too many animals sleep in my bed.

At first there was Max, a fuzzy brown bear,
Who's still my good friend, but he hasn't much hair.

Then came Benny Bunny, Pooze Cat, and Ed Horse,
With Duncan the Donkey and Dog Spot, of course.

There's Jocko the Monkey and Mabel the Moose
And Timothy Turtle and Sasha the Goose
And Wally the Walrus and Winifred Whale
And Percival Possom and Sadie the Snail.

I climb in and seek a soft spot that looks clear,
But my left toe gets stuck in Peg Piggy's right ear.

Then Dick Duck wakes up and lets out a loud quack,
'Cause my elbow has lodged in his feathery back.

Soon Randy Raccoon starts to bluster and wail.
It seems Terence Tiger has pounced on his tail.
And proud Leo Lion begins to complain,
That Roosevelt Rhino has mussed up his mane.

Abruptly old Pooze Cat forgets how to purr.
It seems that Chip Chipmunk's asleep in her fur.

Next Pam Bird pecks Sam Bird so hard on the beak,
That Meg Unicorn rams her horn in my cheek.

Then Millicent Mule brays a mighty "Hee-Haw!"
When Willie Wolf howls, "You stepped on my paw!"

And Sylvia Seal cuffs Claude Fox on the chin
Screaming, "For goodness sake, you're squashing my fin!"

Next Penny the Poodle emits a shrill yip,
When Billy the Goat lands his hoof on her lip.
Fat Wally the Walrus barks out a sharp groan,
As Moose Mabel's antlers poke his funny bone.

Big Elephant Tilly grabs Jocko the Monk,
Shakes him and bellows, "You stepped on my trunk!"
And Beatrice Beaver pipes up with a cry,
As Milton the Mouse takes his paw from her eye.

Next Lillian Lamb bleats at Reginald Ram,
"You're disturbing my fleece, why don't you just scram!"

Then Max the Brown Bear roars, "Madeline Mare!
You've taken my pillow! That JUST isn't fair!"

"Will you all simmer down," I try not to yell,
As Timothy Turtle retreats in his shell.

"No howling, no growling, no words, not a peep,
It's nighttime, it's bedtime, we all need some sleep!"

Soon Moe Muskrat chuckles, Claire Cow starts to laugh.
"Stop making that racket!" shrieks Geena Giraffe.

"Who ruffled my feathers?" squawks Holly the Hen.
Then all of a sudden it starts up again!

With all this commotion, can you understand,
How sleeping in my room just gets out of hand?

Each night you must realize I can't rest my head,
'Cause too many animals sleep in my bed!